Big Bad
Troll

To Liz Bankes
S.P.

For the children of West Mersea Primary School
T.K.

EGMONT
We bring stories to life

Book Band: Turquoise

First published in Great Britain 2016
This Reading Ladder edition published 2016
by Egmont UK Limited
The Yellow Building, 1 Nicholas Road, London W11 4AN
Text copyright © 2016 Sally Prue
Illustrations copyright © 2016 Tom Knight
The author and illustrator have asserted their moral rights.
ISBN 978 1 4052 7825 6
www.egmont.co.uk
A CIP catalogue record for this title is available from the British Library.
Printed in Singapore
60881/1

Series and book banding consultant: Nikki Gamble

Big Bad Troll

Sally Prue
Illustrated by Tom Knight

Reading Ladder

4

Sam did not like being a prince. It was hard to play football with a crown on, and he was always being told off for getting his clothes muddy.

He had to have lots of How-To-Be-A-Good-Prince lessons, too.

GOOD
PRINCING
LESSONS

PROPER
CROWN
ATTIRE

6

'Come and play football,' mouthed Zoe the cook.

But Prince Sam couldn't play
football . . .

. . . unless he could sneak off without
anyone seeing.

The King got very cross.

'How will you be a good prince of
Dull Land if you run away from your
lessons?' he asked.

One day, when Sam was playing football, the Prime Minister came running up as fast as he could.

'Help, help!' he said. 'A big bad troll has moved to Bumpy Town, I mean, Flat Town, and your father the King is in bed with a bad toe. It is up to you to save the town!'

'A big bad troll?' asked Sam. 'But how
am I going to save the town?'

'Well, *I* don't know,' said the Prime Minister. 'You're the one who has had all the How-To-Be-A-Good-Prince lessons. Come along! Quickly!'

'Are you sure it's a big troll?' asked Sam, as the Prime Minister led him to the royal train. 'And bad, as well?'

'The biggest,' the Prime Minister said. 'And as bad as bad can be.'

'Oh,' said Sam. 'And why is it called
Flat Town?'

'You'll find out,' said the Prime Minister,
as he waved Sam goodbye. 'Don't leave
your crown on the train.'

It was a long, long train journey.
'But this isn't a town,' said Sam when
the train stopped at last. 'Those are
sheep. A town is all houses and shops.'

'We have to stop here because of the bridge,' said the train driver.
The bridge was very flat indeed.

'You would have to be a mouse to get under that,' said Sam. 'Oh dear. We will have to go home and not bother about the big bad troll.'

But the train driver shook his head.
'The people need you, Prince Sam,' he
said. 'Don't worry. You can walk the
rest of the way.'

Sam climbed out of the train.

'Why is it called Flat Town?' he asked.

'You'll find out,' said the train driver.

'Don't forget your crown.'

Sam walked along the road. He went round two bends and over three flat fields, and then he heard a sound. *Clunk*, it went. *Clunk. Clunk.*

CLUNK! CLUNK!

'Well, *that* doesn't sound like a big bad troll,' Sam said to himself, and he went over to see what it was.

It looked like a doormat. But Sam had never seen a doormat that said *clunk* before.

'What are you?' asked Sam. 'And why do you keep saying *clunk*?'

The thing jumped in the air, but then landed flat on its face again.

'Hooray!' it said. 'A prince! You will get rid of the big bad troll!'

'I am a prince, yes. But what are you?'
asked Sam.

'I was a hen before the big bad troll sat
on me,' it said. 'Now I am a doormat
with feet. I used to be good at clucking,
too, but now I can only clunk.'

'The big bad troll sat on you?' said
Sam. 'Did you make him cross?'

'No,' said the flat hen. 'The big bad troll
sits on everything. He is a horrible bully.'

Sam soon saw that the flat hen was quite right. He could see why it was called Flat Town, too.

The big bad troll had sat on everything.

FLAT ~~HOUSE~~ FOR SALE

There were flat houses with windows like letter boxes and doors like cat flaps.

There were flat trees shorter than Sam was.

And the dogs had such short legs that they were always getting mud up their noses.

Soon Sam heard shouting.

'A prince!' said lots of very short

people, running out of their flat houses.

'At last! A prince!'

'Hello,' said Sam.

'Hooray!' the people squeaked.

'The prince will make the big bad troll go away!'

'Um,' said Sam. 'Is he a very big troll?'

'As tall as a house!' said everyone. Sam began to feel better. Even *he* was taller than a house in Flat Town. He followed the people out of the town into a very flat forest.

Soon Sam heard another sound.

A stamping sound.

'The big bad troll!' said everyone,
and they all ran away and hid under
the trees.

Sam was too tall to hide under
the trees.

A big round shape came over the hill.
It had two big round eyes and a big
round nose and a big round mouth.

Sam looked up at the big bad troll.

The troll wasn't as big as a house.

He was as big as a tower.

'You look as if you need to be sat on,' said the big bad troll, in a big bad voice.

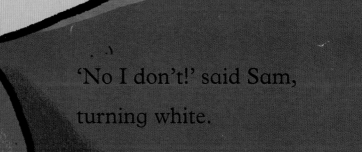

'No I don't!' said Sam, turning white.

But the troll was already turning himself round. Soon his enormous trousers filled the sky.

'Help!' said Sam. 'I'm going to get sat on!'

'No you're not!' said all the flat people, from under the flat trees. 'You're a prince. You'll soon get rid of that big bad troll!'

The seat of the big bad troll's trousers
was getting closer and closer.

'I wish I'd done my lessons,' thought Sam. 'All I know about being a prince is that I'm supposed to wear a crown.'

So Sam put his crown on.

The big bad troll's trousers came closer
and closer and then . . .

OWWWWW

The big bad troll jumped back up
again. The points of Sam's crown had
pricked him very hard indeed.

And before Sam knew what was
happening, the troll was running off
over the hill, howling as he went.

'Hooray for Prince Sam!' said all
the flat people. 'We'll never see that
horrible bully ever again. And now
we're not being sat on all the time
everything will grow tall again.'

'Hooray for Prince Sam!' they all shouted. 'Now Prince Sam will get rid of the big bad dragon, too. Hooray!'

'What? said Sam. 'A dragon? A big bad dragon? Er . . . excuse me.'

'But where are you going?' asked the people of Bumpy Town.

Prince Sam made no reply. He was running back home as fast as he could.

He needed to do lots more How-To-Be-A-Good-Prince lessons.